DELIBERATELY THIRSTY

editor
Seán Bradley

I don't reallly believe that liquor will cure all the ills of our society. But two or three healthy slugs often cure our curious inability to know each other.

Budd Schulberg *What Makes Sammy Run?*

There is a lot of talk nowadays about waste and chemicals which have destroyed everything, but music destroys a lot more than waste and chemicals do, it is music that will eventually destroy absolutely everything *totally*, mark my words.

Thomas Bernhard *Old Masters*

Fuck the County Council! Fuck the the whole fucking lot of them!

Brian Ó Nuaillain

Argyll
p u b l i s h i n g

contributing editors
Eddie Gibbons
Todd McEwen
Hannah Rye

technical support/taxi
Graham McQuarrie

First published 2000
Argyll Publishing
Glendaruel
Argyll PA22 3AE
Scotland

www.deliberatelythirsty.com

Subsidised by the Scottish Arts
Council

THE SCOTTISH **ARTS** COUNCIL

**British Library Cataloguing-
in-Publication Data.**

**A catalogue record for this
book is available from the
British Library.**

ISBN 1 902831 18 7

Printing
Bell & Bain Ltd, Glasgow

CONTENTS

FOREWORD

And My Fate Was Scotland

FATE BROUGHT me to Scotland. I found it cold, its colours softer than I was used to, the birds quiet. In Khartoum, the sun had made everything sharp and smelly. The sun bleached the colours of the washing hanging out in the yard. A special blouse or new shirt had to be hung up to dry in the shade. We spent a lot of time looking for shade.

The view from Sudan is that the entire West is one place; tearless, affluent and all-powerful. In the Blue Nile Cinema I watched American films and British films and couldn't tell them apart. The people looked the same, spoke the same language and behaved in the same 'Western' way, that is they knew better than their parents and rushed around dropping things. After a diet of Hollywood, Scotland was shockingly cloudy, all that grey a mistake.

If I could not tell Britain and America apart in the cinema, I could scarcely tell Scotland and England apart when I arrived. The train from London went on and on, on and on – yes, it would have been quicker to take the Eurostar to Paris. Paris, France, out of the UK. The passengers of the Flying Scotsman were very patient. They ate sweeties and crisps, more sweeties and crisps and the Firth of Forth came and stayed in my memory, the water not blue like the Nile. When the train arrived in Aberdeen, the air was more wonderful than London's summer, fresher. But it was only the different Bank Holidays that convinced me that I was living in another country. To me people in Scotland and England looked the same; they spoke the same language and behaved in the same 'British' way, that is saying please, sorry and thank you all the time.

My alarm at my first Mums and Toddlers meeting – a

mother holding up a biscuit out of reach of her son. 'Say please first'. And then after the poor child stuttered and struggled and succeeded in getting hold of the biscuit, it was 'Say thank you' before he was allowed to gobble it up. All the mothers I had known in Sudan (including myself) were too eager to get as much food inside their children as possible to give any regard to politeness. They coaxed and bullied, waiting for the little mouth to open so they could pop in just one more spoonful. Greetings instead were all important when I was a child in Khartoum. A child had to greet an adult, shake hands, stand up if an adult came into a room. Because I was a girl, I had, in addition to the handshake, to kiss all the aunties whether they were family or not. I got extra points if I smiled and remembered their names. Even among children, greetings were important. If I forgot to say hello to a friend in Secondary school (and that included a kiss as well), she would say with sarcasm, 'Did I sleep last night at your house?'

I moved to Scotland and had to learn new ways in order to get on in life or even just cope. In order not to become superfluous, which could easily happen. The European in Africa is entitled to be there. The African in Europe is *de trop*. He comes and stands back because that is what is expected. Because everything (the locals believe) has already been sorted out and organised, there is nothing really new that he can add. But if we don't add something, we are not living. Put couscous in the English dictionary, Ramadan, pray in a place where people have stopped praying. If we don't add something or change something then why did Fate bring us here?

Gradually I learned to distinguish between the English and Scottish accents. I was able to tell immediately if a sitcom was American or British. It was easy to pick up that it was 'Yes, please' and 'No, thank you', in that way, that order. And don't ask a lot of questions; find out things for yourself. Follow maps, read signs, look up things in the Yellow Pages. This was a reading culture not a speaking one. My shock coming from Sudan where the vast majority could not read and write, to where everything was written down. Everything. I picked up a bottle of shampoo and read 'DIRECTIONS Lather and rinse thoroughly. Repeat if required. In case of contact with eyes, rinse with water immediately.' I asked myself, 'Were there people in Britain who did not know how to use shampoo?'

Sometimes I asked people for directions and they didn't reply just pointed towards a sign. I learned that I was expected to search for signs and read them before asking. (A child growing up in Britain would know this simple fact but for the outsider it has to be learned.) The sheer abundance of leaflets. How to wean your baby, how to cope with a bereavement, how to clean your wok. . . It became a household chore to get rid of unwanted words. In Khartoum, old newspapers were used to wrap sandwiches for school. Buy a book, fresh bread or a leg of lamb and you would get it wrapped up in yesterday's copy of *The Days*. When I was in the University of Khartoum, the student newspaper was hand-written and hung up on a board. As soon as the latest issue came out there would be a rush and everyone would crowd round to read it. We would stand on tiptoe to read the top pages, sit on our heels to read the bottom. Tissue paper was so expensive and such a luxury that I remember sitting in the library with a toilet roll on my desk because I had a bad cold. There were no leaflets in the library.

Yesterday, I saw a man walking in Great Western Road carrying a baby in his arms without a sling, without a pushchair. I was surprised and wondered if there was some sort of emergency. Yet in Sudan, babies were carried in their father or mother's arms all the time. That was their mode of transport, no pushchairs and no slings. Pushchairs and slings were not manufactured locally. The only ones available were imported from abroad and a Sudanese baby in a pushchair was a baby born with a silver spoon. After years in Scotland, I knew that every Scottish baby had a pushchair whether it was brand new, second or third-hand. My eyes had become used to all the signs of Western affluence; dogs in the back seats of cars and furniture in good condition left out on a skip. That man carrying a baby in his arms, without a pushchair or a sling looked unusual, a memory from a faraway place.

When I first came to Scotland I used to wonder why everyone became so happy and rushed outdoors as soon as the sun started shining. I couldn't understand why they went about saying, 'What a lovely sunny day!' It was just normal for me and still too cool. The sun shining – that was what the sun was supposed to do, that was what the sun had done every single day in Khartoum. I couldn't understand why they said, 'Lovely day'. I thought, 'A normal day, finally, after months of rain'. Now years later I began to feel as happy as everyone else and agreed, 'It's a lovely day'. I began to take rain and grey clouds for granted and not sunshine anymore.

I moved from heat to cold, from the Third World to the First – I adjusted, got used to the change over time. But in coming to Scotland, I also moved from a religious Muslim culture to a secular one and that move was the most disturbing of all, the trauma that no amount of time could cure, an eternal culture shock. I left a way of life connected to the source. I moved from a place where death was close and pervading like Scotland's clouds, where sadness was a friend. A life different from the West's. The language was different. 'I will see you next week, if Allah wills it to be', 'You did so well in your exam *al-hamdulillah* – thanks to Allah', 'This is very sad news, may Allah compensate you', 'Thank you for your help, may Allah reward you'. Years in Scotland and I still cringe when someone says, 'I'll definitely be there'. How do they know? How can they be sure? It's smoother to my ears to hear, 'I'll be there *insha' Allah*: I'll be there God willing'.

I found in Scotland very little knowledge of Islam or the Sudan, the two things that made up my identity. What people knew was as accurate as the view I'd had of Britain watching 'Carry On' films at the Blue Nile Cinema. I hid my homesickness. It was my big secret, not to be acknowledged, not to be expressed. I was twenty-seven, twenty-eight, twenty-nine and I had a lovely family but I had to push myself through every day. Back and forth, I went to the GP with various pains and infections. I ate antibiotics. Did I experience racism? I was too busy grieving to be sure.

One day I went to an aromatherapist. She asked me questions and filled up the answers in a sheet. 'Any mood swings? Psychological problems?' 'I'm homesick,' I said for the first time and laughed because I was embarrassed. She put her pen down and looked at me. And because she looked at me, straight at me, she became my first friend. 'That's terrible,' she said, 'I got it when I went to college. Homesickness is living in the past.' She gave me a bottle of Clary Sage to take home. I'm not sure if the Clary Sage worked but her words made a big impression on me. Homesickness was living in the past. I did not want to live the past, I was too young to live in the past.

I searched for an insight, a rationale. Why did Fate bring me to Scotland? Why did Fate take me away from my home? It was a breakthrough when I found an answer. In the pages of a paperback entitled Winter Lectures, simple words written for me. *Everything coming against our desires is only coming by our Lord's will. If we know this we can attain peace and surrender. When we stop fighting, then His will may lead us easily to our destination without trouble or fatigue. Prophets and saints are like this; they reached Paradise in this life. Sometimes I say* al-hamdullilah *my will is not happening. His will is best.*

Leila Aboulela
Aberdeen
February 2000

Friends & Neighbours

LEILA ABOULELA

[Two women are hanging out the washing in their respective gardens.

LESLIE (Scottish) is hanging out large dull coloured sheets and towels. Her actions are brisk and confident. Her washing is hung neatly on the line, in the traditional way; shirts upside down, socks together etc.

REEM (Sudanese) is hanging out children's' clothes. Her movements are slow, hesitant. Her washing is hung haphazardly, jumbled up. When she speaks to LESLIE her voice is subdued.]

LESLIE: He's still away then.

REEM: Yes. He's moved from one rig to another . . .

LESLIE: You must feel there's no point to you being here really, if your husband's away all the time.

REEM [apologetic] : He can't help being offshore a lot.

LESLIE: My nephew's in Abu Dhabi. He's there and you're here. It doesn't make sense, does it? These companies don't seem to know what they're doing.

REEM: We're not from Abu Dhabi, we're from Sudan.

LESLIE: I see, where's that then?

REEM: In Africa, south of Egypt.

LESLIE: Oh Africa. I don't think of Egypt as in Africa.

REEM: It is . . .

LESLIE: This is a nice neighbourhood. You're very lucky to find a house here.

REEM: We are.

LESLIE: No house-hopping here. Everyone keeps themselves to themselves. That's what I like.

REEM: Yes.

LESLIE: Quiet too.

REEM: Yes.

LESLIE: I hear your children running about in the house. It's not what we do here, you know. Children should run outdoors, not in the house. Last night we were watching the television and we could hear them running up and down.

REEM: I'm very sorry.

LESLIE: You can't let them run about the house. How can they run indoors, over the furniture?

REEM: Yes they play imaginary games. The sofa is a ship and they jump . . .

LESLIE: It's not right.

REEM: I'm very sorry.

[LESLIE finishes hanging out her washing and walks indoors.]

[A man appears in the garden. His nationality is irrelevant. He has kind eyes and a kind voice. He is wearing a dark green turban and cloak made of rough wool. Under the cloak he is wearing loose camel-coloured trousers and a long shirt. There is nothing silky or glittery about his clothes but he is certainly out of place in this 90s Aberdeen garden. He is wonderful. When she sees him REEM is transformed, lit up, a different person. She stops hanging out the washing.]

REEM: You've grown up!

THE STRANGER: You've grown up too.

REEM: I like your turban and your clothes.

> [The stranger looks pleased, a little proud. He touches his turban lightly.]

REEM: What do they mean?

THE STRANGER [pauses a little, remembering a past struggle]: I have a higher station now.

REEM: But you used to have wings. . .

THE STRANGER: I did. I miss them sometimes.

REEM: You were a bat and you used to come to me through the bathroom window. You used to fly in through the window and hang upside down from the shower rail. I would be sitting on the toilet, my feet not reaching the floor and I would talk to you for hours.

THE STRANGER: It didn't smell nice – the bathroom.

REEM [laughs]: I'm sorry. I didn't know bats could smell things.

THE STRANGER: Everything had a sharper smell in Sudan than here.

REEM: Everything. Dust and sweat. Watermelons and beans with cumin. . .

THE STRANGER: The necklaces made of jasmines that you used to wear. . .

REEM: They were fun to make, with a needle and thread. . .

THE STRANGER: I used to watch you pushing the needle through the stems.

REEM: Sometimes I couldn't see you but I knew you were there. I only saw you in the bathroom.

THE STRANGER: I spent nights on the roof of the petrol station. The smell of the fumes was enough to get high on.

REEM: Everything had a sharper smell. Soap and the starch in the washing. . . Why doesn't everything have a smell here?

THE STRANGER: Because of the cold. The cold numbs away the smell of things.

REEM: And the colours aren't the same. They're not vivid enough. . . they don't make my heart hurt.

THE STRANGER: It's the sunsets you miss. They don't have the same sunsets here. It's all repressed. Repressed sunsets and repressed smells.

REEM: Why?

THE STRANGER: It would be too much for them here. Too much to bear.

REEM: Just the rain.

THE STRANGER: The only great thing is the rain.

REEM: You like rain. It's generous like you. Do you come from a rainy place? All these years, since I was born, I've never asked where you came from, where's your home.

THE STRANGER: It doesn't matter.

REEM: Why not?

THE STRANGER: We're all passing through.

REEM: You're still secretive. . . you were always secretive.

THE STRANGER: Tell me your news. Tell me a story.

REEM: I don't want to cry. I want to be happy with you.

THE STRANGER: Don't tell me a sad story then.

[Pause]

REEM: I stand on the Umdurman bridge and look down at the water mixing together. There is dust in the wind and the smell of cars, the hot gleam of the sun on their bumpers and again on the water below. Two rivers meet under this bridge. They have been running for miles, over different countries with different names

13

and different terrain. Now they are tired. Tired of running alone. If I look, if I listen closely I will know this giving in, this bowing down, this soft giving up of independence. One Nile is dark and heavy with silt, one Nile is blue and transparent. Under the bridge, their edges blur. They breathe in and start again. It's a long journey to the sea, deserts and pyramids, palm trees, lots of palm trees. I will tell you why the river runs to the sea, I will tell you – to rest. To rest. When the river reaches the green sea it doesn't need to run any more.

[Pause]

Here in this house, I hear things sometimes. Noises from home. I hear the call to prayer coming from a mosque. It comes to me in the central heating pipes. It comes in the sound of running water from far away. It says, come on, come on run, leave everything and pray. It pulls me like the sea pulls the river.

[Pause]

At night I dream that I am a child back home. I am wearing one of my daughter's dresses, this dress [she holds one of the dresses hanging on the line] and I am playing on the porch. There are large clay pots on the porch, bright red, with cacti and bougainvillea. I keep away from them because if I touch them, they will hurt my hand. There are tiles on the floor. With a piece of coal I draw lines and boxes to play hopscotch. I write the numbers too, every box has a number. I live in my dreams, they're like honey. Then the children wake me up in the morning. Their voices wake me up. They put the TV on very loud or they run around the house. They come and jump on my bed. My son holds a knife, right up to my face. . .

[THE STRANGER looks at her in surprise.]

REEM: A knife and a jam jar against my cheeks. It's the cool glass that wakes me up. He also holds a slice of bread and the crumbs fall on the sheets. He wants me to spread jam on the bread. It's for his breakfast. I should get up early before the children and get breakfast ready for them but I'm dreaming. I'm inside the dreams. . .

THE STRANGER: You dream of me.

REEM: Yes. Like now. Do you feel it when I dream of you?

THE STRANGER: It's like being tugged in, pulled in. . .

REEM: . . . into another world, another life.

THE STRANGER: Lush. That's how it feels with you, lush.

[Pause]

REEM: Do you still go swimming in the sea?

THE STRANGER: I'm going now. Most of the time the sea is too calm. [There is resentment in his voice or sadness.] Much too calm. The food I get is too sweet, it's always sweet. And when I touch something it's like foam, it isn't real. [He pauses, then his tone becomes more reflective, resigned.] But this is my trial and my exile. Water smooth as a prayer mat, not one single cloud in the sky.

REEM: Tell me something nice before you go. Something I will keep and it will be mine.

THE STRANGER: On the Last Day everyone will be with his beloved friend.

REEM [slowly, tentatively]: Everyone will be with his beloved friend.

THE STRANGER: . . . on the Last Day. . .

REEM: . . . I will be with my beloved friend.

[LESLIE comes out of her house carrying a deck chair and the *Press & Journal*. She cannot see the stranger. REEM goes back to hanging up the clothes.]

LESLIE: It's turning into a nice day.

REEM: Yes, it's nice.

LESLIE: It was dark earlier on – I thought it was going to rain.

REEM: No it didn't rain.

LESLIE: There's new people moving in across the road. Got two little ones, twins.

REEM : Twins, that's nice. Where are they moving from?

LESLIE: Down south. [Pause] All sorts of folk coming into Aberdeen now. They think the streets are paved with gold.

REEM: Do they?

LESLIE: They do so and this is a good area, this is. Everyone wants to move here.

REEM: Yes. . .

[LESLIE sits back on the deck chair.]

LESLIE: A bit of peace and quiet before your children come back from playschool, eh.

REEM: I'm sorry about the children.

[LESLIE opens the newspaper and speaks without raising her head.]

LESLIE: What a carry on in your part of the world! A right mess.

REEM: Yes.

LESLIE: You can thank your lucky stars you're here, even with your husband gone half the time.

REEM: Yes.

LESLIE: They just can't seem to sort themselves out, can they?

REEM: No.

ENDS

The Handfasting

IRENE LEAKE

1
'This is how we learn to draw. Observe
acutely the flayed figure, écorché, the cast of a
common criminal. Consider anatomy, notate with
rigour the body stripped, stripped again, the noble
pose, the plaster dyed the shade of juices from the
walnut, of dried blood, burnished, set on a plinth
as elevated as any military monument.'

After the black rain, I begin to draw.

I draw   Severed Autumn Stalks,
I draw   Montbretia, Flaming Fistfuls,
I draw   Fire, Tapered Candles.

•

2
Dad, I've drawn this for you.
He adjusts the focus of the projector, and tells us,
'My son drew this, for me, it's good, it's funny, isn't
it? He was good at cartoons, look, that's me, he's
drawn me in this one.'
Dad. I'm dead.
'Please, sir, I have made one for you too. See.' I am
wet, I take a drawing from beneath my jacket, the

paper torn from an exercise book gives off a brief warmth which my chilled fingers cannot feel. He turns in my direction, looks down. He sees a child's picture, of people running, red, raw, something trailing behind them, he sees me, a woman. He will not take the drawing, controls his speech, 'You are not a child.' That was before he came to know me.

•

3

From the window his young son propelled another paper bird into the air, that was the last of the one thousand, it cruised in clear skies. The people on the ground scattered, as if they were Inuit racing after supplies dropped from a plane, casting off their sealskin parkas onto the melt snows of the tundra.

He too was passionate about birds, birds of metal with fine engines, that looked ugly on land, so beautiful in the sky. Yet his child born in peacetime would not survive, he had contracted a terminal disease and would die, having barely entered adulthood.

The child ducked his head back inside to the bedsit, and watched the old woman shake out the nightdress as she prepared to fold it, pink against paler skin. The old woman had slept briefly yet soundly as usual, and had commenced the day with vigour. Those night hours which she did not need for sleep, she passed in the company of books from the library, thick plastic protecting the illustrations on the covers, light murder mysteries for the most part. She stowed these beneath her bed. 'Nan, what's it made from?' the child asked as he reached out to the billowing cloth, his soft fingertips against the sheer material came to rest on a seam far

stronger than necessary for the garment, parallel
rows of stitching sealed the well-turned raw edges.
Through the material he heard the reply,
'Parachute silk.'

•

4
The young man remains silent, smoothes
his hair from his eyes, leans forward to focus the
lens beyond the blur of fresh snowfall. The district
is familiar enough, as he imagined it to be, the
school run, the village beneath the deep green of the
conifer slopes. Heavy snow must have fallen
suddenly, before the wind had time to pick up, the
snow has settled upon everything equally. He can
see signs that the villagers have made their usual
unhurried preparations, split and stacked wood,
hung ladders and tools in place beneath eaves,
battened down shutters, to get themselves through
to the other side of winter. I pass across his field of
vision, I am here, not only in his imagination; he
will later acknowledge that I have fulfilled his
search.

The snow muffles the atmosphere, yet as I plough
through it, the beat of my heart is amplified as it
swells beneath the layers of protective padding.
Wind directs the snow now, squalls slash against the
waxed paper of the umbrella, my bare hand clasps
the handle, my arm is held fast to my chest, as
always, to protect the drawings beneath.

•

5
I sat in the low nursing chair, and began.
'It was the assistant who detected that the camera
was still loaded. So we sold the camera, the rest of

the equipment too, the son would never be able to use it again, and we left the film to be developed, it was of an old style, paper-backed, wound onto a long metal spool. His father had given him the camera, it was one he'd used during the war. We returned to collect the prints, but at the back of our minds we were thinking that it is said that in this month the ghosts of the departed return to us, we go back to our birthplaces to dance with them, then the dead souls depart in small boats made of paper and grass, they float down the rivers, with lanterns to guide them, and out to sea. He had only exposed two or three photographs, that was all, they showed a winter scene, snow, no-one about. The remaining negatives had been blank, and doubtless it would have displeased him to know that we had wasted so much of the film, we ought to have finished it.

But what could we have photographed, the bonfire, the neat piles of life drawings singed, smouldering? What *would* we have photographed? I remember that I placed the snapshots in the dish that I keep on the kitchen counter, the one with the fresh lemons that I squeeze into hot water to make the first purging drink of each day, the dish shallow, stoneware, fired with blue flowers, winter pansies. I saw that the snow in the photos had taken on a sallow tinge, from the fruit, and only then did I notice that there were faint tracks through the snow. And beneath those tracks there would be bare earth, where feet had worn a pathway too, through summer grass. The young man could have risen from my table one evening and entered his darkroom, he would have agitated the fluid in the tray beneath the red light, he would have seen the shadows emerge, he would have known to manipulate the pincers with care, to lift the print with precise timing before it darkened and was lost, the image of my passage through the snow. But he had no need of the photographs now, he would not lay down his cutlery, for it is I who would serve him, ladle more rice into his bowl, we would eat together.'

I stopped, and drew the basket of wool close, picked up the stitches I had dropped, and continued to knit the baby's shawl. I pointed out that you would only be able to tell that one half of the shawl was stained a duller white if you looked for the discoloration, on the diagonal which marked the widest part, the last row I had knitted eighteen years earlier, at the time of the contamination. I found it easy now to complete the shawl for my next baby, decreasing by a few stitches on each row.

•

6

I judge the wind direction then lower my body into position, not far from me children play, scooping out channels with their spades. The breeze travels up my legs, cool, as I desire, and the weight of my pregnancy disperses into the sand. I narrow my eyes to gaze at the glint of sun upon incoming waves, the wave which breaks closest to me does not seem normal, it is heavier, disturbed. The gray mass recedes, then returns, drawn inshore, it swells and I recognise what it is, the carcass of a dead dog, its innards inflated by the movement of the tide as if it were drawing breath in its sleep.

•

7

A hand of a man glides toward me, I am asleep but do not rest, the disembodied hand proffers a card, between fingertips softened by a white glove. I recall that there are members of the police force who are required to work in water. Close inspection of their diving gloves reveals that two areas, on the pads of the thumbs and along the index fingers, have been worn away in the course of their duties, they trawl through viscous sediments, searching by feel for any resistance, which could mean that they had located bone, a limb.

Again the cards are dealt, and it is I who must interpret, I thought somebody else would do that. The face of this card carries a faded impression, of a man at sea, lounging at the helm in summer uniform. The camera shutter had closed, the exposure had registered his tedium. When he was based at the test site, he had been given special clothing, and had been instructed when to turn away. We had received no such instructions, we awoke to sunshine, and were selected because the cloudless sky above us enabled the most precise dispensation of their load. We had registered that moment as a dream. News of the surrender will skim the water towards him, his breast will swell, they will turn the ship round, and even when he is an old man he will feel the same arousal when he recounts this moment, when he was free to return to his loved ones.

He is my husband.
I am his third wife.

COLM QUINN

The Terms of War & Peace with the Carlins

I

All year round a tall hedge divided the terms
of War and Peace with the family next door;
partitioned the familiarity of our gardens and kept us
separate, yet familiar and at bay in times of siege.

For ours was an alliance of a short distance, forged because
we were neighbours: the peace dependent on the orders
of our Mothers, who were half-the-time enemies,
                                        half-the-time allies
and widows to the evenings in the absence of dull husbands.

On days when association between us was an offence,
our shared hedge became a height; the holes which were
used as easy entries to play became passages to defend
whenever their numbers poked through.

The hedge, a blessing for their disguise: a net over which
they volleyed- and a hurdle over which we returned-
their daily deposits of shitey nappies that they parachuted
over in the night, as anonymous parcels of spite.

II

A shared need to divide the empty boredom of the bright
                                        nights
kept us guessing and listening as to how the Carlins were
                                        coping
without us, kept our Mothers irritable and eager to sweep
                                        their paths

when no emergency presented itself as an excuse to meet and
make up.

For their's was a friendship of conspiracies, spanning years
over
talks, treacherous with barbs aimed homeward.
Each woman pretending while brushing to ignore and not
need
the other, but begrudgingly awaiting a call
or a beckoning nod, enough to forgive for.

As they stood conversing, supporting their weights on the
gate,
they policed the peace between them with talk of news,
an ushering in of hushed views, whispered freely
on the loose lives of many there.

Then, parting that evening with forgiving tut-tuts
and ack-sure assurances that they'd never name from
who they heard it from first.

This was the sign for us to lift the blockade of our gardens,
to reopen entries, to refresh the longing of our divided play.
Our Warring Mothers returning home, informing
uninvolved husbands
that the embargo on the borrowing was over:
a calling off, a ceasefire on the flight of shitey nappies.

Joey Budgie Barry & His Beaky Wife

I refused to call him *Joey*
On the grounds that it made a
Grown man sound like a budgie.

An aging punk rocker with
The hair or plumage
Of a rare tropical bird.

Only the size of an ostrich,
Joe could've balanced on a perch
And hopped from her hand over to

A swing and a tiny toy bell.
For this, I call him Joe in order to show
The man his dignity.

But last night his bossy wife served
Me with an eviction, with two weeks to go,
Screaming as a last point

That his name was Joey, NOT JOE!
So when I leave I will buy Joey some
Cuttlefish in the hope

Of him pecking back his beaky wife
And pin a note to say,
Carmel, feed Joey two times a day.

The Intricacy of their Alibi

My big sister was his little victim;
ready-made, kept-in-place
and ever fearful of him.

I imagine you that Sunday,
Hungover yet eager with
Ready-made admissions of guilt.
First to wake, forgiving all
To save a home already built.

He decided to rise and left you lying,
Repaired things broken but felt
Obliged to bathe you Geraldine;
Dress you then drill you
On the importance of lies.

We couldn't tell when you came here
Fronting a loyal union with him,
Excusing the rosy stamp of violence
Where he'd bullseyed you on Booze again.

We didn't know that day.
He was supportive yet suspected-
Innocent as the accident
That left you no scars,
Only a waxen yoke of bruising.

Da, *you* even thanked him for bringing her home.
Her head, cradled and tilted back,
Her wound was cold pressed
As our rage was displaced
In the intricacy of their alibi.

Eve: Anatomy of a White Woman
(extract)

KATHERINE ASHTON

AT FIRST I thought that everything would be all right.

It begins with a sleep, like a fairy tale. It begins with the first sleep, the sleep of a winter which must become spring. The day is calm, uncoloured. There hangs over everything a waiting, a hesitation, an immanence.

Eve stands up, puts down her book, crosses the room and looks out of her French window. The gardens beneath her balcony throw up their ancient smell. It is March, and after the tremendous freeze trees unlock their branches and the earth allows a first meek movement of breaking bulbs.

She has only to wait.

She recrosses the room, picks up her book, lies down once more on the settee. The room is neutral; the panelled wall redolent of pinewood, the beige carpet, the leather upholstery, all offer synchrony. She lies lulled by their single voice.

A venturing ray of winter sunlight penetrates the window pane and slides forward towards a tall plant standing by the antique dresser. Dark jungle green accepts the alien equivocally and then repulses it. The terra cotta pot warms briefly as if recalling southern origins.

Pale light floods flowing oak, ignites a pool of aqua-opal porcelain and reaches on towards the fireplace where it explores the dark cusps of a pinecone, and suddenly retreats as if defeated by a promise of devouring.

It does not reach Eve, outstretched upon the settee, watching and waiting.

But the waiting must be over.

How long has it been like this? For how long has she lain here? For how long has she watched while the sun entered uninvited, explored the bevelled edges of the pinecone and known its many throats?

She will not today burn it. She will not now dust the china serving dish garlanded with blue roses, with the faint tint of former faded appetites. She will not touch that tenderly turned wood which leads her dream always into Flemish forests. Today she will not clean her windows.

Instead she will lie here, becoming lighter and lighter until only the scent of her perfume is left; lighter and quieter until she is quite dissipated and dispersed and not even her memory remains.

My memory, which others prefer even to my truth.

And her truth expands, and rising dispels itself into droplets and is gone.

●

Between the strangely autonomous earth, with its stirring, its crepitation and its own inhabitants and the lifeless blue firmament above, there moves this singing, surging in which I am swept along.

And always this discrepancy, a dysharmony between the present and my now, possibility and plausibility, certainty and the shifting moment. I am in the act of attempted super-imposition like a mating bird, a half- blind man, determined to unite images, to map myself onto the moment.

And arriving always only to find myself too late. I see from the way that others look at me that they do not mind. I see they are content that I hold no sway over the time and cannot bind myself unto its content. Sometimes I think that they rely upon my absence and upon the promise of my presence, never fulfilled.

One clear morning I appeared upon the face of the earth and I was perfect. There was holy violence in the set of my shoulder and sacred virtue in the muscles of my leg. I strode forth without fear and met man eagerly, face to face.

We stood together, side by side, he glorious in his own nature; I lovely in my own. Where he was straight, I curved. When he laughed, I wept. We flew forward in a clean arc; I trembled at his departure and at its consequence. There was no discrepancy between us.

But when the blow fell it severed us. All around me there was chaos, clamour, dread. I could not cope with such calamity for I could not feel that I deserved the curse.

There was no more joy. Birds trilled no longer in the trees. Anenomes bled themselves to death behind me. All succulence, all sap-fed green was gone. I knew that we would never more twin like grass-hoppers beneath the trees.

I turned around and faced the place from whence we came and felt a tearing firey pain lifting my entrails from their bed. A red flow fled from me leaving me appalled upon its farthest shore. I bit my fist, but self-inflicted pain was suddenly remote, a distant possibility.

I could bring nothing to bear upon myself. I crouched and waited while some part found a cave, fumbled there like a scarred, exsanquinating thing which seeks its final sanctuary.

The sucking, dragging, rushing inner agony sustained and fed itself. I saw there was no reason, no justice, no escape. I crouched, waiting while the man moved off into the torrid sunlight. I knew the hair rose on his neck; his skin boiled, blistered and bled. I smelled his fear.

He did not turn around to look for me, but lurched on forwards, following his thirst and searching for a sign. He scanned with searing eyes our far horizons,but he was alone.

And when he came back at last with food for me, I could not meet his eyes. They were as moulten marbles.

We dropped. We fell like fellows, each through his separate track, each doomed, discredited. I felt my ears stopped with his accusations and in reply I gushed forth impossibly from my own exits while grimly he contained himself around the promise at his centre.

All of our meetings have been mismade since then. I cannot tell precisely why. It has to do with this inner absence and a strange hunger that cannot be fed.

I crouch and expel myself within my cavern, smelling the wetness of its ancient walls, recoiling from the sweating rock, knowing in shame the limits of my safety.

Sometimes an early agitation admits itself here, scorching these barbarous walls like some unknown sun, lovely and forbidden. And for a moment I hold to the heat, I burn, I hurl myself towards its core. It feels like something forgotten against my skin and hunts inside me poignantly for that which I have lost.

I have grown to know and welcome that; that harsh awakening, that clarity, that brief illumination, ending always in eclipse.

That fire as all-consuming as a pain, unfocussed as a photograph, ignited in the tiny form who steps indomitably, freshly forth, casting behind her like a caul the doorway to her parents' home, its towering rhododendron, the oddly posing woman.

The blossoming bush disintegrates; its petals separate and fall like withered smiles upon the path and secret, glossily new leaves emerge to bear their first burden of winter snow.

A little girl steps out, encased in a red siren suit, her cheeks aflame, beneath her chin the sharpening chafe of skin just now pinched in a too-hastily closed zip.

She knows a world of lightening rage imprinted and replaced by fairy footfall and the hungry robin's flight, the soft spread of her muffled hand.

She sucks at earthy nothingness, bites through the wet wool of her mitten until her fingers feel, and strokes the strange antennaed mosses quiet in the wall.

As hunger hollows her within, the glittering, yielding universe she's found increases, variously gouged and ploughed, but ceaseless. She totters forward, falls and finds, though lost, the world has caught her safely to its breast.

She waits, astonished, frozen, still, but still no mother comes.

●

It is four o'clock. Eve gets up, stretches, crossesd once more to the window. A tightening surge invades her belly. She stops, accepts it with her hand, waits for the rise, the plateau and then the fall. She takes her hand away.

Down in the gardens which fill a triangular space between the backs of blocks of flats, cats stalk, sleep, sullenly search. As Eve watches a man emerges onto a balcony in his shirt sleeves and drops three empty beer bottles into a yellow plastic crate. Their clattering disturbances rise onto the air like crows.

Eve's glance sweeps across the triangle to the opposite side where identical balconies protrude, bearing like indiscretions evidence of hidden lives: a dustbin, lace underwear drying amidst last year's geraniums.

I must not look!

Twin plumes of steam arise irresolute from the two chimneys of a power station behind the flats.

And there is the unoccupied one, below, behind its bare, blind windows, haunted by the kind with whom she has populated it on other empty afternoons. And there is Bob Dylan, pinioned to a half-open door, crying out into the rosy lotus night; a pink paper poet tethered in vacancy.

He accuses me of beauty and of his solitude.

But wait. She is there.

In the flat above: the woman in the window, whose face I cannot see. And she is brushing her hair. She brushes her hair in the mirror. Golden filaments fly upwards, each lit, each driven from its neighbour by a sudden charge. She draws the brush through and through again, generating dispersal until it meets the unresisting air, then plunges it back into the mass again.

She stops for an instant, steps to one side, looks down into the gardens, seems not to see the cats, the derelict pigeon loft, the saffron-souled crocuses, and steps back once more behind her oval mirror and begins to brush again.

Sometimes Eve tries to find her in the street. Once, in the bakery along that block, she saw her in the crowded shop, her face stamped like a cameo upon a chocolate box, her hair on fire amidst the snaking ribbons, her cheeks glittering like chrystal fruit.

Gazing up and down the long glass shelves marching with petit four, studded with Parma violets, her eyes ablaze, she bought coffee gateaux with hazel nuts, kiwi fruit tart, deathly meringues; crumpled white meringues that fell in like puffballs, showing their charred white centres exuding ash.

And if I spoke? What should I say?

Eve paid the proprietess, swallowing a smile that left her eyes as blank as sugar almonds beneath their heavy lids; a tiny, poisonous movement of the mouth, a baring of small white teeth slightly smudged with red.

I should begin very gently. I should say, 'Hello, I think I know you. You are the lady who brushes her hair for many hours before her window.

'You are, I see now, neither young nor old. No, please do not run away. Please do not be afraid. This afternoon, you see, when the sun passed you, I thought you were extinguished and only your hair remained, burning like a halo.

'And so many questions occurred to me. I wondered how long you had been there and whether you lived alone. But of course you do. And in your bedroom, behind the dressing-table whose mirror I can see, there stands a huge brass bedstead covered with a patchwork counterpane.

'Now I can see how carefully you do your eyes and with what a wonderful assortment of subtle shades. I can see the small white pots, the lotions and the creams, a chiffon scarf, a dish of pot pourri upon your dressing top. How lonely you must be.

'Don't be afraid of me. I saw you. You were brushing your hair and I thought of a candle flame at the centre of which is nothing although that is its hottest point. Your face was pale and featureless and I thought of the celendine which flowers when the swallows come and perishes when they leave.

'I thought of golden petals and a fecund centre; the speechless beseeching of the celendine. Or of the barren snowdrop, her head bowed modestly toward the earth. Of these. and of so many other things.

'You seem to me – forgive me if I am wrong – to be waiting, preparing for something or someone. And yet the days and weeks go by and still you appear, forever at your window, brushing, brushing. And I wish that you would stop.

'I wish that this tireless effort would cease, for it is nothing. It has no purpose. Although now your hair glitters and stands like a crowd of stamens, no pollen rises resolutely on the air, no hopeful dust waits to be wafted out of your window, later to land judiciously.

'You have misplaced your true nature. You have misplaced your direction and your reason. You have forgotten your own name. I want so much to whisper it back to you, but you will not stop brushing, brushing your hair.

'You move always in an empty circle. Between the elements your flesh motions eternally and beside it turns your soul, unseen, a remote satellite, an unclaimed star. Deep in its own darkness tracks your unnamed planet, terrible in its lost majesty.

'Put down your brush.'

'Take in your thin white hands the brass worlds of your bed and hurl them out into the wastes of space to turn there endlessly. And take that other darkness to you.

'Then wrap your patchwork with its million stitches around your body. It will be warm and luminous with cataractous light. Wrap yourself up warm and go. Go out.'

●

Inside the cold dark taxi cab Eve hugged her book of stories. In her hair was a blue velvet Alice band which pushed the lank brown locks behind her ears. on her feet were night blue satin slippers with turned-up toes, like those she had seen in pictures of the Arabian Nights. She had been promised the slippers as a special treat for coming home. She could just discern the glimmer of their gold embroidery through the darkness.

And behind her was the hospital. Eve felt very light and weak, very white. The hospital had almost obliterated her. She knew that she would never recover her equilibrium. She sat very still. The little orange story book felt warm, slightly rough in her hands. The interior of the taxi smelled of dusty leather and of alien bodies.

'Are you all right, darling? Are you warm enough?'

No, mummy, I am terribly cold and light and white, like a snowflake in the darkness.

The nurses put all the children on pots at certain appointed times of the day. They would all be sitting on top of their beds, facing one way down one side of the long ward and the other way up the other side, boys and girls.

Eve balanced on her pot and waited for this torture to be over. The edges of the pot bit into her bottom. The slightest movement on her part would overturn them both. a thought that paralysed. How could they do this to her?

She was sick bright red blood all over the sheets before she'd had time to call for nurse, and that was the second time. Her body betrayed her constantly. She listened to the nurse's complaint horrified.

She lay there speechless, for days or weeks or months. She saw the back of the child in the next bed each time that they were potted and that was all.

She was put in a huge bath. She had to sit at the back, and in front of her with his back to her sat a black boy of about her own age. She had never seen a black body before.

She looked at his ebony skin with its roughnesses, its

palenesses and its soft silkiness, and saw how its blackness disappeared, wavering beneath the water. He is completely black, she thought, and I am completely white. What does that mean?

They both got out of the bath and stood shivering, naked, on the brown linoleum floor. The nurse rubbed Eve hard with a rough white towel until her skin burned while the black boy watched unmoved. She returned his stare, stripped of fear, of origins, of her own name.

A letter arrived for her and one of the nurses read it aloud, sitting on her bed. It was a long typewritten letter, telling a story about a little girl. It was from her mother. The nurse said how nice it was.

Eve wondered where her mother was. Her mother, her father and her little sister had all receded to a very great distance and were barely perceivable to her now. The pain of their absence had been replaced by a void which protected itself from further loss. A dark, solid line had become drawn around it; a boundary which defined her self and cut it off from the outrages offered her each day.

The nurse finished reading.

'Isn't that lovely? Isn't your mummy clever to write you a story?'

Eve saw her mother's face, minute, through the far bars of a cot. The face was perfect in every detail, but disembodied. It appeared between the wooden slats at the bottom left hand corner of the cot and advanced slowly, growing larger all the time, towards where she lay.

She held her breath as the face got bigger, nearer; she opened her mouth, stopped in the foyer of a scream. She lay very still. The face ceased.

'It won't be long now, darling. We'll soon be home.'

Eve hugged the little orange story book. Her feet and hands were very cold, very stiff, very thin, reaching into the darkness of the taxi cab. The Alice band bit like ice into the tender flesh above her ears.

She waited for weeks in a darkened room upstairs in the new house for her fever to subside, smelling the peppery heat of her own skin and isolated in a strange unquestioning. She could no longer follow her own fortune.

Inside the flyleaf of her story book she watched her father's handwriting float above a picture of the Sleeping Beauty, encroach upon Aladdin with his lamp: "For Eve-out-of-hospital love Daddy and Mummy." At last the pencilled marks stood still.

She wobbled beside the bed while her mother wrapped her in a rug then led her down the stairs. Her father was home from work, the room acrid with cigarette smoke, defined in every detail by his presence; the solid set of his chair, the closed sheen of his spectacles, the absolute impassive law which issued from the radio.

Eve bent her being to the comprehension of this state which found its voice at six o'clock each evening; a wider order which deserted them anew each day to fall into a timeless trance of muted masteries.

She walked like a sonambulist beside her smiling mother, counting the identical doors that opened off the bear-kept pavement like lairs, not stepping on the lines.

Inside a neighbour's house, snuffing the scent of territory not her own, she circled wary in the orbit of a foreign stare, of lifeless objectivity.

'Why don't you play, you two? There are plenty of toys to play with. Go outside and play in the garden.'

Her mother came and found her there, exploring the sticky sweetness of a hollyhock.

'What ever made you do such a dreadful thing?' she asked. 'What came over you?'

Eve waited while her mother stared into the silent space she made. Suddenly, she took up Eve's wrist and bit into the flesh until it bled.

'There! That's what it feels like!' she declared. 'That's what you did to that poor little boy. Now go and say you're sorry.'

Back in the known enclosure of her early evening room Eve heard the front door slam, her mother's tearful reportage, the radio, a heavy footfall on the stair.

She opened her book. At the bottom of the opposite flyleaf, out of his reach, reclined a little mermaid, combing her hair in limpid innocence before an oval mirror.

•

Eve turns abruptly from the balcony, stoops by the dresser, touches with her fingertips the dry dark earth which crowds the terra cotta pot. She fills a jug with water quickly at the kitchen sink, returns and watches its greedy welcoming.

She passes on around the room, oblivious to her surroundings, intent upon redeeming trailing tradescantia, pale spider plant, shocked at the arid pathos of a fern, until she reaches the kitchen once more relieved as of a crime.

Soon all of this will find its vindication: the shining sinks, the ample surfaces, the gaping washing machine. Soon the waiting will be over, as meals are over and the last parsley-speckled juice scooped up in jetty shell, the last bread broken, the final drop of golden wine distributed.

It will be over. She leans forward, the kettle in her hand. An aluminium sky crumples, altered and recoiling from twin eructations of steam.	❏

JOHN SYMONS

Soup Chef

I hang one thumb in the notch of your shoulder,
the other on your hip.
This is no clinging for dear life:
I must envelop you light
as a cheesecloth shift
and feel your heat, your heartbeat
and their rise, their fall
while like a politician
or a soup chef I exist
only in the stir I make.

Eventide Homes

Eventide homes in upon the beach
and six hours on will shuffle seaweed coils.
Even surf survives a little, boils,
expiring over worm shafts. Ding dong leach
of salt up river, sweat and urine down.

Red cliffs crumble. Some unpicking stitch
releases sand to join the backwash, sud
in ruffs round grains that tumble till the thud
of breaker. Gulls goose-step the fever pitch
of slated roofs. Oh, Purgatory town.

Phoenix

The cottongrass flashes
its rabbit tail warning:
pitch here no tent
or turn to tarn your groundsheet.

Yet the peat
like two cupped hands
holds water where would be dry rock,
holds all life where the bare stone would rule.

This is the true phoenix
the slow wet burn of blade and twig
to carbon almost diamond pure,
to ingots cut to bank warmth in our black houses,
to the candle flames of autumn:
cowberry, blaeberry, cloudberry leaf.

Under the Trees

Of all things true in the world,
none more than these:
more it changes, more it's the selfsame thing;
after the rain
it rains
under the trees.

Gentleman's Literature

ALAN BISSETT

MRS WHITE, the nurse next door, was the stuff of my teenage dreams. Since reaching that age when your dreams end up voided on your bed-sheets, that is, I'd begun noticing her not as that nice lady who worked at the hospital and occasionally dropped in to see my Mum, but as six foot of skin, flesh, legs – blonde hair flaring like flame on her shoulders. The whole summer had been spent peering like a mole from my bedroom window, trying to memorise the sight of Mrs White like a bronze idol, lotion glistening on her endless, paradisal curves. Whenever she bit into anything, I heard the music from the Flake advert.

"It began with a P. . ." Cameron stuttered, "Pentboy or Playhouse or something."

"And it's definitely her?"

"Positive, man. The Readers' Wives section. White knickers one minute. . . off the next!"

"Can you not just bring your brother's copy in?"

"Frank's? You kidding?" Cameron's brother was an ex-paratrooper, an intimidating mass of indian-ink snakes rippled on the sea of his biceps. Cameron had told me Frank's philosophy on the rite of the naked image in a boy's education: "Gentleman's literature," he called it proudly, patting his groaning collection. "Like getting a tattoo, know?" I can guess how he developed the arm muscles.

Mrs White was finally going to be mine. Conquered. All it would cost me was two pounds fifty and a brass neck.

"Are you not coming in with me?" I whined, the moment of truth drawing near, like a hearse, like buffalo charging, but Cameron just grinned, absorbing every second of my knees-crossed discomfort. "Hey, I'm just here to point you in the right direction! Divine messenger, ken? Listen, I'll get you in an hour outside Virgin." And with that he disappeared, like a mysterious monk in a story who warns the hero of a looming danger.

Virgin. Cheeky sod.

You understand, of course, I couldn't walk into any of the shops in Stirling to buy a copy – scandal spreads like epidemic round our way – so Cameron and I had taken the day off school and the train to Glasgow. I hated skipping school and I hated calling Mum at work to lie that I'd developed flu, but the one sin had started begetting a whole host of others; from the second Cameron had dropped that naked image into my head I'd felt this sex-crazed serpent hiss and writhe and grow there.

I was still naïve enough to think that just because I was in Glasgow the whole thing was going to be easier, but this, I frantically reminded myself, spitting nervously at the pavement, was something that Men did – tattoo-clad Diet-Coke Break mechanics and the like – and so I closed my eyes, picturing Mrs White one last time with her thumbs hooked in the waist-band of her descending white knickers. . . then I was in there, battering the door open like a western gunslinger!

The young girl behind the counter looked up at me.

I made sure to close it quietly on my way back out.

RS McColl's across the road had a man serving.

Now, I figured that if I made it clear that there was purpose in my purchase, that I was being honest, grown-up, business-like about the whole thing, they were apt to respect it, get the message that for this gentleman it's No Big Deal, a regular fellow making a regular transaction. Not like the ones who come in, shuffle about, and pretend they're not looking at the top shelf! *They're* the perverts!

So I went in, shuffled about, and pretended I wasn't looking at the top shelf.

I went to the fridge, took out a can of Coke, and gently appraised its temperature.

I picked up a copy of *New Scientist*, and read an article about nasal polyps.

The shop assistant's blank face was pushed into his Daily Record, and so, sure the coast was clear, I raised my eyes to the top shelf.

There was enough to stock an army barracks for a year. I seemed to have stumbled onto the largest collection of 'gentleman's literature' a newsagent could hold without putting a red light on the door. Their exotic names collided into one . . . fiestapenthouserazzleplayboyescortclubnudewives. . . and I reached up, casual, as if merely plucking an apple from a tree or screwing a lightbulb a little tighter. But as that tantalising angel-glimmer descended, every time I had seen part-way up Mrs White's skirt at Mum's parties, or her bending down in the garden, or even fiddling absently with her bra-stap getting out of the car, collided into one bright image that came sharper into focus the nearer my hand got to that shelf, and just as my skin touched the skin of the orgasmic model on the cover of Escort, a voice, alarming not inside my head, said:

"Should you not be in school, son!"

At first I thought it was God, and I was dead.

Then I thought: The Rector. He's come all the way to Glasgow to catch the doggers and here he finds his potential school dux feigning illness to work himself into a sweat before the largest display of nudity he's ever seen, and I will be expelled, disowned by my sanctimonious parents, branded a goat-worshipping Satanist, abandoned to a future on street corners with men in dirty macs. I formulated my excuse – I was reaching for *Trout-Fishers Weekly*, sir! – then, solemnly, turned to face my doom.

It was the shop assistant, whose resemblance to Graeme Souness I hadn't noticed before. His moustache bristled with authority a foot away from my face. I could smell things on his breath: coffee, perhaps blood.

"I said: should you not be in school. Son."

"Eh. . . In-service day," I attempted, fumbling my hands back into my pockets. I was hoping he'd take pity, remember when he was a horny, young buck himself. But no. He looked at me like I was a puppy that had pissed on his carpet. Must have been a teacher at some point.

"Well yours is the only school then. Besides, that stuff. . ." he pointed at the place of my crime, ". . . isn't for you."

"But, eh, I know somebody in them."

He opened his mouth, snapped it shut, squinted at my apparent lie. This pale, spotty youth was obviously not the type he imagined hanging out with glamour models in his spare time. "Look, it doesn't matter if your Auntie Jeanie's the guest editor, son, that's not for lads your age. What age are you anyway? Fifteen?"

"Fourteen," I confessed.

"Well there you go then. I cannot legally sell you such material." And he crossed his arms, solid as the Sphinx, just daring me to argue this legal standpoint.

The next place elicited the exact same response: icy stares, accusations, even a threat of the police. And the next. Any sane schoolboy would have cut his losses right there and trudged back to school with a forged sick-note. But I had been infected. The sight of that shelf glistening flesh above me, the promise of Mrs White secretly spread somewhere among them, had me entering the fourth shop with breathing now shallow, rigid, horned-right-up. The woman at the till (about the same age as my mother) clucked innocently around with jars of sweets, unaware, I could see, of the desire machine that had entered her presence. She glanced up as I approached, perhaps sniffing with some honed female danger-sense my arousal, while I grabbed without hesitation the first magazine on the top shelf and started flicking through, man-like and felt quite sick.

This was a sight not normally revealed to adolescent Terry Pratchett fans like myself. The punch-line of a joke I'd heard at school unfolded, one I hadn't even got at the time: Right enough, Eve, you've no teeth down there. But your gums are in a terrible state. . .

The magazine was slapped onto the counter, the woman-the-same-age-as-my-mother turning from the sweetie-jars, but the money was down before I could even register the disgusted look set in her face. What do you look like underneath that sweater, I remember thinking, trying to fix the picture in my mind for later, the whole of her sex mine now, stripped.

Offended, she took my coins without a thank-you, as if I was caring. I didn't even care if I had the captured Mrs White in my pocket or not, because it was at this point, quite seriously, I began to fear for my penis.

Out of breath I charged back to Virgin Megastore and Cameron, who smirked as if I was a smuggler delivering booty.

"You get her?"

"I hope so."

"Well hurry up, the train's coming. And so am I."

I didn't hear a word Cameron said all the way home. The magazine glowed in my pocket and a lump grew in my jeans, which I felt sure everyone on the unbearably crowded train could see. I tried to distract myself, looking out of the window at fields and trees and animals and the glory of creation and that carry-on. But as we shunted nearer Stirling: knickers waving on washing-lines and sunbathing women all floated back into view. Readers' Wives everywhere.

Into the house, and we slammed our victim onto the table and started rifling through her insides, the searing under my clothes like rising lava (the minute Cameron left they would be off, discarded, useless to my intoxicated, burning condition). "There she is!" he squealed, pointing to a white shape near the centre pages, Ahab sighting Moby Dick, "I don't believe it, man, it's her!"

It was one of those moments that define your life.

Even as I experienced it, I felt a new self being formed, the person I was seconds before being shed. A hoodwinking destiny comatose on the tracks, that I was never going to avoid, that I'd hurtled towards. And crashed against.

She stared back from the glossiness with narrow, lust-filled eyes.

My Mother.

My mouth dropped open, my hands fell slack, and I moaned like a wounded dinosaur.

"I know," Cammy marvelled, hogging the page. "Gorgeous, isn't she. . . ?" ❏

HELENA NELSON

Our Lives As Sleeping People

I talk all the time – undeciphered snatches;
you are a world of silent swallows,
snorted scuffles with air-filled pillows.

I plunge to the depths, ready to interview
crystalline X-rays and fish-stars and fear;
you linger safe just below the surface

where you peer through grey, unworded tedium
and wait – without knowing you wait – for me
to scissor into the air and check

in my wet-suit primed for ordering matters
that you have not drowned
that you are still breathing.

*Note: Jo Shapcott has a poem called 'My Life Asleep' of which she says:
"I began to be curious about who or what I was when I was asleep. What was
my life like as a sleeping person?"*

The ravell'd sleeve of Ma

It wasn't just a hobby. Herbert's Mum
knitted him woolly sweaters by the score.
'Give us a hug, Ma,' infant Herbert begged
but she tossed him another jumper, acid green,
dragging the dreaded wool over his eyes.
At eighty-four the aging matron died,
leaving her grown-up son some minor bills
and ninety-seven sweaters, scarcely worn.
A loose thread started him: a little pull
and he was off, *un*knitting jumpers, winding
up his grief like a man possessed. Then as
the house filled up with wool re-skeined
he even began to sing, just like his mum
when casting on. Abandoning golf and squash
and stamp-collecting too, he wound bright globes
around and round and round and heaped them up
each evening in the hall. He'd always thought
his mother's love was strange; at last he saw,
inspecting his collection (no mean pile),
she'd given him her all, and all was balls.

Thumbscrew

Poetry bores me.
I think I will become a poet
so I can bore people.

Inflicting boredom's not so far from pain.
I have always been interested in pain.

I had never thought of poetry like this
till now. I am less bored than I was.
I think dinner can wait.

I have written a lovely poem about a thumbscrew.
Let me show you my new metaphor.

W.L.WHEATLEY

Requiem Warhola

Pop's pop: deadcat hair, albino nose
lobotomy stare, mismatched clothes
rendered a pop bottle, soup can
Brillo box, Elvis and Marilyn
totems of the marketplace hung
and galleried for the rich to buy
guyed by Pop's audacity
camping out on Madison Ave;
burghers boggled – is it a joke? –
the empty box, the painted can
cost so much more than A & Ps!
What should I paint you polled the public;
Paint what you love some lady replied.
You painted money, a portrait of cash.
High Art is moola? Somebody laughed.
Yes! But of course! You've got it, Warhola!

I never paint, you coyly fibbed,
it wasn't a lie, the silkscreen did.
Print the spoof, sell the scam, get up
on the wall any way you can.
Reflect the gloss, the shine, the chrome
the tinselled dots, the cheap and thrilling
blatant spot the artificial
light will find; the brutal smoking
carbon arcs sears a swath of
glittering litter and disposed debris
through the pullulant, purulent GNP:

resplendent in the radiant glare
a face, a form, so brightly lit
it must be someone truly great:
for fifteen minutes of its own
it's being known for being known.

A Factory rack of ravelled fabrics
warped and woofed, stoned, drugged and drunk
your wretched huddled teeming freaks
yearning to be known, displayed their
bare demented ornamented
psyches on the cool avid lapping
lens for us to see the putre-
faction of another human
been. *Nihil obstat* the blankest
gaze when you set your sideshow
pretties in the pit, razors
slashing wrist to wrist, a dripping
nose under star-painted eyes
cicatricose veins, crushed butts, splin-
tered nails, a limp dick, a ductless tit.
Such enervation! A gas, a goof!
Twisted, banal, traduced, bereft,
jerked off, pissed off, seduced and left
twenty-four times per second per
second. *My inspiration,* you
silently writhed, *don't stop now, she'll*
die on film and keep me awake!
She shot you twice, one of your whores
SPAT SPLAT that wasn't a bore.

Ultra Violet, Billy Name,
Edie, Baby Jane – exhibitions
like the fiction Warhol from
unpainterly McKeesport
the Czech coal miner's son so
fey and fated by biology
bleached bland and gaunt, a shy and
mincing nervous breakdown hid

in Mama's arms, eating chocolates
in her lap, turning pages
of her movie magazine, rapt in
poses of the stars, tracing
Bette, Mae and Cary, Doug and
Ron and Joan in bright crayola:
the panting pix in reigning rays
the queens and kings of the republic!
Their cartoon babies graze museum
walls stillframed in iridescence:
Marilyn, Elvis, Campbell
and Coke, even Mao – what a joke!
You played us on your pianola
clever boy that young Warhola!

Dandy Andy, the popsicle top
the Pontifex Maximus of Pop
a speculum from sternum to spine
a glaze of mercury on glass
a scintillant mirage who showed
us what we saw, no more, no less,
no less. You had a vision of,
not art – *a man's name,* you yawned –
but glory's trompe l'oeil: fame.
A lidless eye, a breathless sigh,
an airbrushed cheek and mute de-
cachinnated grin: Pox populi!

Lhude sing requiem Warhola:
apathy, accidie, anomie,
ataxia, aphasia, america.

A Year in the Life
of the Queen Mother's Hip Joint

IAN HUNTER
COURT CORRESPONDENT

JANUARY:
HIP JOINT IN REMOVAL TRAUMA SHOCK
Buckingham Palace today announced that the Queen Mother's hip joint was comfortable after being removed in a two-hour operation. Hundreds of get-well cards and messages of support have flooded into King Edward VII Hospital in central London. One bouquet of flowers was accompanied by a card which simply said: 'To the nation's favourite hip joint. Get well soon, Tony.' The hip joint is expected to be released after ten days' rest and a good clean and polish, possibly leaving the hospital by a side entrance to avoid media attention and a pack of dogs which have begun to gather.

FEBRUARY:
HIP JOINT CREATES BONE OF CONTENTION
HRH or not HRH? That is the question which has plunged the Royal family into another constitutional crisis amid speculation that the Queen Mother's Hip Joint will have its HRH title removed and be simply called, Hip Joint, Princess of Birkhall, after the Queen Mother's Scottish residence. During Prime Minister's Question Time yesterday, Left-wing MP Tony McClumsky called it madness that the public purse should have to bear the cost of looking after a bone and suggested that the hip joint be ground down and fed to the cows to give them something decent to eat for a change. While the debate rages,

the Hip Joint's staff, led by Lady-in-Waiting Dame Ethelia Haberdashery, remain tight-lipped about their future.

MARCH:
FERGIE MAKES HER MOVE
Staff of the Queen Mother's Hip Joint have been reported to be distressed by the rumour that the Duchess of York is pressing the Queen to allow her to display the Hip Joint at her new home in Windsor Great Park. It is believed that the Duchess sees the Hip Joint as a veritable gold mine and a sure-fire way to utilise some of the fourteen bedrooms in Forest Lodge by hosting Royal Surgeon 'theme' nights where members of the public will compete against each other to earn the right to remove a replica of the hip joint from a wax model of the Queen Mother.

APRIL:
FERGIE DEVASTATED BY HIP JOINT TOUR
Sources close to the Duchess of York report that she was seething after the Queen Mother's Hip Joint was ordered by Buckingham Palace to accompany the Royal Barge, *The Lucky Duck*, on its tour of British canals before it is officially decommissioned at the end of this month. The absence of the Hip Joint effectively scuppers the Duchess's plans to apply for Lottery support for her Royal Surgeon theme nights at her home in Forest Lodge, Windsor, as there is every chance that the Hip Joint will remain with *The Lucky Duck* after it is decommissioned.

MAY:
GLASGOW WINS BARGE, BUT REJECTS HIP JOINT
Glasgow Council today defended their decision not to accept the Queen Mother's Hip Joint after making a successful bid to be the resting place of the Royal barge, *The Lucky Duck* which is being decommissioned and is expected to become a popular tourist attraction. The barge will take pride of place in the re-opened and upgraded Caledonian Canal, but there is no place for the Hip Joint in the Council's plans as revealed in a statement released yesterday: 'In these times of shrinking financial resources Glasgow Council cannot afford the security

costs necessary to protect a royal bone. Nor could we afford the associated costs of keeping the Hip Joint in the lifestyle it enjoys. We also feel that continued media and public interest in the Hip Joint would have a detrimental effect on local residents due to the presence of members of the paparazzi.' Buckingham Palace have refused to comment on the Council's decision.

JUNE:
HIP JOINT HOMELESS SCANDAL
Traffic was brought to a standstill outside Harrods yesterday as hundreds of people crowded to catch a glimpse of the Queen Mother's Hip Joint and its Lady-in-Waiting, Dame Ethelia Haberdashery, as they busked outside London's leading store. 'Yes, there have been casualties,' the Lady-in Waiting quavered bravely, referring to the reduction in the number of the Royal Bone's staff in the last few days. 'Two staff have taken menial positions at a nearby Burger King, while another two have sold some of their organs for illegal transplants, and several were eaten by homeless people living in cardboard boxes on the South Bank.'

JULY:
FERGIE LANDS 'HIPPY' DEAL
The Duchess of York, self-proclaimed manager of the Queen Mother's Hip Joint, announced yesterday that she had secured a deal with the Japanese computer giants, Shogucci, to produce a computer game of the adventures of the Royal Bone and a resurrected Jack the Ripper called Hip Hop Jack's Back Slash. The deal, worth one million pounds, also includes a series of cartoon adventures about, Hippy, the Hip Joint and a range of soft toys, a cyber pet in the shape of a hip joint and a series of illustrated books to be written by the Duchess who will also appear on American talkshows to promote them. 'I know what it's like to feel like a Royal outsider,' the Duchess said yesterday. 'Hopefully this deal will enable the Hip Joint to lead the sort of life that I enjoy.' 'Over my dead body,' replied Dame Ethelia Haberdashery.

AUGUST:
BEATLES REFORM FOR BENEFIT CONCERT
The world of popular music was astonished by the news that the Beatles have reformed to perform a summer benefit concert for the Queen Mother's Hip Joint arranged by Dame Ethelia Haberdashery in a last desperate attempt to keep the Hip Joint out of the clutches of 'that woman'.

SEPTEMBER:
AUSSIES SAY NO! TO POMMIE HIP JOINT
Plans for the Queen Mother's Hip Joint to become Australia's first president look unlikely following remarks made by Bruce Kolinski, leader of the All Pommes Must Die party. Kolinski told reporters at the party's annual convention/barbie that it was bad enough that the President might be a Sheila, but there was no way it was going to be a Sheila's bone. 'Don't get me wrong,' he said. 'I've got nothing against the Queen Mom, after all the old bird likes a bet and a tipple, but there will be no bone in charge of Australia, just the same as there will be no Abos in the new Parliament, and no women if we can get away with it.

OCTOBER:
HIP JOINT IN MY BOX SHRIEKS UPSET MUM
It wasn't a deep fried rat. It wasn't a deep fried mouse, but something resembling a deep-fried hip joint that caused mother of three Cheryl Melvin to lose control of her car and spin off the road and into a tree when she dipped into the box of Alabama Chicken Fries that sat on her passenger seat and pulled out a piece of chicken shaped like a hip joint.

'I'll sue,' Mrs Melvin said from her hospital bed. 'This American multinational megacorp must be taught a lesson. The Hip Joint is a cultural icon. One of the most important bones of the twenty first century. They can't get away with trying to cash in on its popularity.'

NOVEMBER:
HIP JOINT IN SPONSORSHIP DEAL COMPROMISE
American fast food giants AFC announced yesterday the signing of a major sponsorship deal with the Queen Mother's Hip Joint

and the launch of chicken pieces in the shape of the Royal Bone. Commenting on their out-of-court settlement with Mrs Cheryl Melvin, the company did admit that a product prototype had slipped though their quality control systems and they regretted any offence that had been caused to the public. The new product will be called 'Bones in a Bucket' and adverts featuring the Royal Bone with her Lady-in-waiting, Dame Ethelia Haberdashery, playing 'Dem Bones' on the spoons will appear on television next month in time for the annual Christmas rush on deep-fried chicken products.

DECEMBER:
HIP JOINT HORROR AT PRODUCT LAUNCH
Onlookers could only stand and watch in horror as the Royal Bone was snatched out of the hand of Marvin G Leadbetter III, UK Chief of Operations for Alabama Chicken Fries, and swallowed whole by a Great Dane that had gate-crashed the launch party of AFC's new product, Bones in a Bucket. 'I smell a rat,' Leadbetter said angrily. 'That dog was not on the guest list.' Visibly shaken, Leadbetter confirmed that they would be keeping a close eye on their competitors for any indication that a similar product is coming on to the fast food market. 'Let's face it, people. That bone is going to go through that dog pretty unscathed, and it's still our bone.'
'I can't believe it's gone,' Dame Ethelia haberdashery muttered to the first aider who put her in the recovery position after she had fainted. 'It meant so much to us. We will never see its like again. That bone was a saint.'   ❏

Stations of the Heart

Eddie Gibbons

1 902831 11 X £6.99
from bookshops and mail order
tel 01369 820229
www.deliberatelythirsty.com

HILDA MEERS

On the Cliffside at Ballard Downs

On the cliffside at Ballard Downs
Froth of star-strung blackthorn blossoms
Crowded in clouds of white.
Across the bay,
Grey seamist shroud, sea split asunder
By shining footmarks of the striding sun.
The tilled and seeded fields are full, heavy –
Leap of wind, the path uphill,
Diversion of seabirds that perch, fly, float,
Squat Old Harry rocks, call –
April 1st: this bright moment shared with you.

'Two Climbers are Reported Missing on Ben Nevis'

Cold climbs and classic rock:
I see your upward gaze intent;
I know, do not need reminders from
the well-loved photographs,

how your pulse would quicken,
your long fingers flex
their eager anticipation of the found hold,
the route up the Ben a thread of delight
unfolding in the quick of your brain.

With canny carefulness,
equipment well checked, wind and weather studied,

you'd work it out so well; choosing a route,
the links of desire, for you like a problem in astrophysics,
deciding, which other scarce-trodden, little-known way.

I, too old to make that climb, staid where no wind-blown
snow skirls, yet felt with you an utter clarity of mind,
joined with the wild surge, throb of exultant blood.
Glad at the summit of your gladness -
as if our thoughts clung,

we hung together on the mountainside
roped in a phantom connection through
mere shreds of severed umbilical cord,
the ropes and belays
of our lifetimes' lifelines;

and so, although at last
the searching helicopter found you, seeing
red stains spread wide across Ben Nevis' snow –
because you loved cold climbs, Brian
I don't regret I didn't say, don't go.

Propage

PAUL WELSH

CHARACTERS:
SISYPHUS – A smarmy smooth-talking cut-throat.
MANAGER –The misguided salt-of-the-earth.
CHORUS – The voice of conservative habit. The fear-ridden,
cowardly corner of every psyche.

[The sales/reception area of a warehouse. Drumming his
fingers on the counter, the MANAGER looks bored. At the
front of the stage, facing the audience, two women are sitting
on chairs and drinking tea. A variety of large objects are
scattered around the stage: an anvil, hammer, red silk cloak,
inflatable finger. The women turn to each other and speak in
a fearful, conspiratorial way.]

CHORUS 1: Whit? Ye huvnae heard? Guilty. The man's been
shackled. 'Enough's enough', judge said. 'Yer history.'

CHORUS 2: Who?

CHORUS 1: Who? I cannae believe. . .Where huv ye been. . .
Huv ye got a brain? . . . Sisyphus! Merope's husband.
Her dad's Atlas. . .

CHORUS 2: I love men wi broad shoulders.

[SISYPHUS enters walking extremely slowly across the
space. At this point, he exists in their imagination. In his
hand, SISYPHUS is holding a sheet of computer print-out,
the embodiment of some grim, distant bureaucracy.]

CHORUS 1: Are ye listenin to me? Sisyphus hud a herd o cattle in Corpach.

CHORUS 2: Corpach?

CHORUS 1: Corinthe! Whit am ah sayin. . . ?

CHORUS 2: Ah dinnae really know. . .

CHORUS 1: Well listen to me! Autolycus pinched a few of his cows. Sisyphus soon put a stop to his thieving. . .

CHORUS 2: Aaaaye. . .

CHORUS 1: Then he shagged the man's daughter. . .

CHORUS 2: Anticleia!

CHORUS 1: A while efter, Salmoneius pinched the lad's kingdom.

CHORUS 2: Nasty!

CHORUS 1: So Sisyphus shagged his daughter tae. . .

CHORUS 2: Tyro!

CHORUS 1: She mothered him two lovely weans.

CHORUS 2: Aaawww. . .

CHORUS 1: Then killed them both.

CHORUS 2: Naw!

CHORUS 1: All because Sisyphus didnae love her.

CHORUS 2: Ye cannae blame her.

CHORUS 1: Terrible but it's no the worse part. . .

CHORUS 2: He murdered three folk. They wir just oot walking.

CHORUS 1: People dinnae know whit's good for them. . . He lied tae Zeus as well.

CHORUS 2: Naw! It wis Persephone.

CHORUS 1: Yer right. A wee bit confusin aw this. . .

CHORUS 2: He blabbed a heap o divine secrets.

CHORUS 1: Extorted the gods. . .

CHORUS: [In unison.] . . . had a fuckin riot. . .

[As the gossip ends, SISYPHUS reaches the counter.]

[Stage lights up.]

[A beat.]

MANAGER: [To CHORUS] They're still using dot matrix. Stingy old bastards.

CHORUS 1: Dae people never change?

MANAGER: It's difficult when yer D. E. A. D.

CHORUS 1: Dark Eclipse Also Deluge? [Struggling.]

CHORUS 2: Dismal Ex Admits Deceit? [Struggling.]

MANAGER: Dire Ending After Delays. [Correct with a flourish.]

[The MANAGER laughs. SISYPHUS remains silent. The MANAGER notices.]

Enough ladies. The man's no amused.

[The MANAGER takes the paper from SISYPHUS.]

[Quietly] Yer no deid yet wee man. Dinnae worry.

[Silence.]

[Loudly] Tae Be Collected by Sisyphus. One extremely heavy boulder. Preferably massive. . . Zeus.

[Silence.]

[Loudly] You've no got the best name around here. . .

SISYPHUS: [To MANAGER.] I can only see my grave. . . Gossip means nothing to me. Pass over my eternal burden.

MANAGER: [Smiling] I could listen tae that patter aw day.

CHORUS 1: [To CHORUS 2] Do ye feel a wee draught in here?

CHORUS 2: [To CHORUS 1] It's turned awful cold.

SISYPHUS: [To MANAGER] Hand over the rock. The more we speak, the more life seeps away. Do you not feel it?

MANAGER: [To CHORUS] Are ye hearin this chat. That wis a total cracker. . .

CHORUS: [in unison.] Wit?

SISYPHUS: [Sharply.] The rock!

[Silence.]

MANAGER: [Backtracking.] Ah'm forgettin maself. There's mair important things to get on wi.

CHORUS 1: Get a move on you.

CHORUS 2: He's always gettin dazzled by their patter.

MANAGER: [Searching.] Some paperwork to complete. . . Yer a busy man! Here we go. . . [Finding another sheet of paper.] . . . Now dinnae get me wrong, we all respect heroes and stuff. Christ, where would the staff be without ye? I've only got a job because o ye. Cannae knock that.

CHORUS 1: Dinnae like aw this chattin.

CHORUS 2: Dinnae like it at aw.

MANAGER: Quiet youse! Ah'm sortin him out!

CHORUS: [In unison.] And Careful!

MANAGER: [Ignoring] Now dinnae feel bad about yer fate. Somebody hud tae land the shite ending.

SISYPHUS: But the end is only the beginning. Where is the rock?

MANAGER: [Searching] No point rushin son. Dinnae worry aboot the future. It's no worse than workin here wi this pair of old cunts. Arses glued to those seats. . .

CHORUS 2: Cheeky bastard!

CHORUS 1: Yer no so bonny yersel!

MANAGER: Ignore them. Ye hud a laugh. People noticed ye. The Gods hud tae sit up and huv a gander in yer direction. Yer somebody. . . That's more than anybody will say about me. . .

CHORUS 1: Say Sisyphus is a killer.

CHORUS 2: Say Sisyphus chops people up.

SISYPHUS: [Smiling] That was never proven.

MANAGER: [Politely] And that's legally binding. . . Ye better sign.

[SISYPHUS signs the form.]

MANAGER: Hang oan a minute. I'll go and check whit's happenin wi yer rock. . . Dinnae you bother moving, ladies. I'll fetch it myself.

[The MANAGER leaves the room. The CHORUS make no attempt to move. SISYPHUS starts to inspect the room. Unsettled, the CHORUS intermittently glance back at SISYPHUS.]

SISYPHUS: Trapped on this boring planet, dull people can often shine brighter than the stars. Wouldn't you agree?

CHORUS 2: Oh aye!

CHORUS 1: No doubt about that!

CHORUS 2: Couldn't agree more!

[Little shuffle.]
[Silence.]
[SISYPHUS keeps walking.]

SISYPHUS: A profitable business?

CHORUS 1: Widnae know. . .

CHORUS 2: Dinnae ask.

SISYPHUS: Good perks? Good bonus money?

CHORUS 2: Well . . . you know . . .

CHORUS 1: . . . competitive.

SISYPHUS: Good tea breaks?

CHORUS 1: Couldnae be longer!

CHORUS 2: Cannae complain.

[Silence.]

SISYPHUS: And you know who I am?

CHORUS 1: We aw know . . .

CHORUS 2: . . . everything.

SISYPHUS But do you know me?

[Before the CHORUS can answer, the MANAGER reappears.]

MANAGER: [Cheery] Well, at least I know who ah'm no, if ye know whit ah mean. Ah'm no a hero.

SISYPHUS: Perhaps . . . but the Gods despise me. You're lucky. You should be happy. Everyone is your friend. Thor. Jason . . .

MANAGER: [Flattered] And I've got ma favourites. Cyrano wi his big . . . [Gestures]

CHORUS 1: [To CHORUS 2] Dinnae say another word!

MANAGER: [Boasting] Don Quixote! Mad fool, but whit a laugh.

CHORUS 2: [To CHORUS 1] Whit a nightmare.

MANAGER: [Revelling] Carryin that big lance . . .

CHORUS 1: [To CHORUS 2] He might need one himself.

[Silence.]

SISYPHUS: My shadow has passed across this earth. . . Will people remember Sisyphus?

MANAGER: No remember ye? Ah'm sure they will. The staff here certainly will. Won't we GIRLS?

[Silence.]

MANAGER: I've always wunnered whit it's like tae be a hero. Tae charge aroond the world daein things wi stuff. Aw the talk. . . [Pause.] Every day, I pray tae gods frae aw o'er the place. But nothing changes. Here I am. Signing out gear tae the greats. Giein them a pat for saving us. . .

[Silence.]

MANAGER: I hud Hansje Brinker through once. . .

SISYPHUS: Who is Brinker?

MANAGER: He's efter yer time. He stuck his finger in the dyke, so I says tae him, 'Hansje, it's dark, the sea is crashing o'er the wall, Holland is balanced on the edge o a life-threatening catastrophe, people are dying aw o'er the place. What made ye stick her finger in there?' He turns and looks at me. He waits. Thinks aboot the question and says 'Either ma thumb or ma country was going tae stop the flood.' His country wis worth more tae him than his own finger. What can ye say? A noble man.

SISYPHUS: Brinker.

MANAGER: Takes aw sorts you know.

[Silence.]

MANAGER: What's in yer bag then?

SISYPHUS: My personality. My memories.

MANAGER: Gie us a look.

[The MANAGER starts pawing around in the bag.]

CHORUS 2: [To CHORUS 1] He was always a nosey bastard.

CHORUS 1: [To CHORUS 2] Curiosity, eh. . .

CHORUS 2: See where it gets him!

CHORUS 1: I don't want to think. . .

CHORUS 2: I know.

CHORUS 1: Curiosity, it's a terrible business. . .

CHORUS 2: I know.

CHORUS 1: Yer so right. . .

[The MANAGER looks up.]

MANAGER: [To SISYPHUS] Some state, eh? Yer no expectin tae carry this about. . . it weights a tonne.

SISYPHUS: Aaaye, it's been a load o trouble. . .

[SISYPHUS mimics the MANAGER's broad accent.]
[The MANAGER laughs.]

MANAGER: No regrets, wee man! This could've happened tae anyone. We're aw very sympathetic, ye know. The afternoon you cornered Anticleia. . . 'On yerself wee man!'. . . Whit a day! The sheer cheek. Four cheeks. Great stuff. I'd trade baith arms tae dae that. . .

CHORUS 1: Dinnae talk shite!

CHORUS 2: Yer ower feart.

CHORUS 1: Big diddy.

CHORUS 2: Ye like yer wee job. . .

CHORUS 1: . . . ower much.

MANAGER: They're spoutin a load of shite. Ah wid so, youse!

CHORUS: [In unison.] And Naw ye widnae!

[Silence.]

MANAGER: [Furious] Well how can ah. . . ? The shop needs lookin efter. And youse as well!

CHORUS: [In unison.] And See!

[Silence.]

SISYPHUS: I could never survive this life.

MANAGER: Whit?

SISYPHUS: [Smirking.] Sweat. Misery. Routine. . . Working here must be awful. How do you manage?

MANAGER: Come on. It's not too bad. We have plenty o adventures tae. Just last week, Thor's hammer fell off the tap shelf. Wi aw the fury of Valhalla, the beast clattered doon on the flair. Whit an experience!

[Silence.]

SISYPHUS: [Ebullient] You're not serious. Tell me you are joking. Could a man impress a child with this story, never mind a woman?

[The CHORUS snigger.]

MANAGER: My wife disnae speak tae me anymore. Well, no much. The job's very demanding. I'm here every day. Long hours. I hardly see her.

SISYPHUS: [Sensitive] A man must see a woman every day. In every way.

MANAGER: How many moons have turned since we last thundered under the silk sheets of passion?

CHORUS 2: He's no shagged. . .

CHORUS 1: . . . for ages.

SISYPHUS [Profound] But a man must always 'shag'. Can a man be a man otherwise?

[Silence.]

MANAGER: I better fetch yer stone. . .

[The MANAGER leaves the room.]

SISYPHUS: [Shouting.] Make a woman feel something. Then the world will remember.

[Silence.]

CHORUS 1: Dinnae look.

CHORUS 2: Dinnae say anything.

CHORUS 1: He might go away.

CHORUS 2: Dinnae look.

CHORUS 1: Dinnae say anything.

CHORUS 2: He might go away.

CHORUS 1: Dinnae. . .

[The MANAGER returns.]

MANAGER: Whit dae ye suggest, then?

SISYPHUS: What do you mean?

MANAGER: Ye know. . .

SISYPHUS: Nothing. What can I say? The adventure is over. I have no answers.

MANAGER: But you'll be remembered forever.

[Silence.]

MANAGER: Ah've got an idea.

CHORUS: [In unison.] And Oh no. . .

SISYPHUS: Tell me.

MANAGER: When I hud a look roun the back, the stane wis almost finished. It's big but ah'm no as skinny as you.

Maybe. . . [Pause.] . . . maybe it's time tae jump o'er the fuckin counter. Maybe it's time tae get a grip o somethin. Get fuckin involved!

CHORUS: [In unison] And Madness!

MANAGER: Nae mair! I huv had enough o yer bleetin, moanin, miserable, tripe-ridden faces. Can ye no just shut it? I'll gie the boy a hand and push the rock tae the top o the hill. . . Zeus just says get it o'er the back [Waving the computer print-out.]. No hang about till the bloody thing erodes. When ah'm done, I'll come back and meet you. It's Friday, we'll go oot on the randan and huv a good laugh.

SISYPHUS: Are you sure?

MANAGER: [Sarcastic] Naw!

CHORUS: [In unison.] And [Worried] Naw?

[Silence.]

[SISYPHUS waits.]

MANAGER: Whit?

SISYPHUS: Nothing. . . A kind man.

MANAGER: Right.

[After picking up a coat and shuffling some papers on the counter, the MANAGER walks towards SISYPHUS. He hands a set of keys to him.]

MANAGER: [Nodding.] Here's the keys. Keep an eye on those two.

[The MANAGER exits.]
[Silence.]
[SISYPHUS picks up his bag and walks towards the door.]
[Silence.]

SISYPHUS: The rain has started. . . The man will never reach the summit.

[Silence.]

CHORUS 2: Scotland, eh. . .

[Sitting, the CHORUS strain to see the MANAGER.]
[Silence.]

CHORUS 1: Could take him forever.

[Silence.]

CHORUS 2: Cup of tea?

[Silence.]

[Lights down.]

THE END

Scottish Snow

CARL MACDOUGALL

The Editor
The Scotsman
108 Holyrood Road
Edinburgh EH8 8AS

Sir:
It is daily becoming more than ever obvious that our country cries out for reassurance that the drug alcohol's place in Scottish life and letters remains secure, and that it continues to exert a profound influence upon our national literature and learning. We need to know the many novels, stories, plays and poems started in pubs, not to mention the innumerable Great Scottish Novels which lie wasted in the howffs and stews of Byres Road and Rose Street, did not wither in vain.

The great body of our literature mentions intoxication, hangovers, shakes, sweats and other drink-related maladies. Most writers are clearly imbibers. The finest poem of the last century is even named after a bibulater, our National Bard is established in popular memory as a drunk and no Scottish novel would be complete without the sensitive lad o' pairts who takes to the drink. Since Robert Louis Stevenson wrote that Dr Jekyll took the potion and 'reeled as though drunk' it has been assumed that the place of drink in Scottish literature was forever secure.

This can no longer assumed to be the case. The thrill of

illegality threatens to remove the honest drunk as surely as it has changed the social habits of society. Consider the implications if the trend continues. The courts will suffer, for all drink-related crimes will be removed from the statute book. No more charges of urinating up closes, pends or wynds; spewing in the street will be a thing of the past and breach of the peace a rare occurrence.

And if such charges are dropped, what will the legal profession do with no drunks to defend? They are the perfect example of a professional collective who have developed skills which will be lost to society if this abominable trend is allowed to continue. Publicans will go out of business; but apart from being bad for the economy, it is unsocial. The idea of going for a fix and a curry is ridiculous. But even more is at stake. Addicts are usually stay-at-home, humourless individuals prone to depressive introspection, therefore the entire Scottish song-writing business is threatened. To obliterate alcohol from our musical tradition does not bear serious consideration, yet that is the prospect. Surely we can see, the town addict will never replace the local cheery drunk with his merry quips and a pocketful of change for the bairns.

What, I ask, are the so-called Scottish Arts Council doing about the problem? Are they even aware of its existence? It was they who allowed the decline in Arbroath Scots to continue when they were well warned of the consequences, something many find difficult to forgive.

No less a person than a former editor of the *Scottish National Dictionary* has remarked that the Inuits have more than 50 names for snow. Consider the following list of Scots words, in common everyday usage:

wastit	swacked	fozie
miroculous	craftie	hertie
blootered	lumed-up	tosie
stotious	roarin	tovie
steamin	chippit	stotin
wambled	bleezin	swittlin
swash	blebberin	fankled

mappie	cornt	poopin
smeikit	stavin	styterin
fankled	molassed	troosert
drucken	moidert	bladdert
drouthie	manky	bleezin
bellowses	fuddled	sappie
slochened	mingin	soopie
meisled	fleein	roarie
pished	galraviched	reezie
boggin	blin	paloovious
legless	blitzed	niddle-noddled
jaked-up	guttered	capernoitit
fittered	minced	fu

There are, you will notice, more than 50 words here recorded and others I could mention, mashed, rubber-leggit, wreckit spring to mind, nor have I even considered the lexicon of phrases in everyday parlance, such as Daein the stiff-leggit walk or Waltzin the alkie two-step, a variety of words and phrases which describe not only the condition of drunkness, but states of that condition.

With a view to preserving a way of life, I have recently begun recording my own experiences. Tentatively titled *A View From The Rooftops* (see *Lanark* by Alasdair Gray) the story opens in a Highland glen, where young Angus is listening to his grandfather's tales. The old man tells him how the snows came and with them the strangers who took the glen with fire and sword, banishing the people to a foreign land across the seas. The old man enjoys a hearty dram from his own still, gives a dram to the laddie, who swears vengeance on those who drove his ancestors from their wee bit hill and glen. His grandfather, nodding by the fire, tells the child of a curse his great-grandfather put on the House of Invercullion: a yellow-haired laddie will be their downfall.

Meanwhile, Morag gets ready for the school display. She is excitedly looking forward to the evening where she will perform the sword dance before the minister and elders. Her best friend Catriona will also be there. Catriona's granny has a cottage in the Highlands where the girls are to spend the summer. Catriona has told Morag of Donald the ghillie, Callum the blacksmith and Auntie Heather who keeps the local shop and makes the most delicious scones you've ever tasted, and she thrills at the very idea of a place like Invercullion, where everyone waits at the pier for the boat to arrive and helps unload the cargo. She has also told her of the Fairy Knoll, deep in the heart of the Cullion Glen, where strange events are said to take place at midnight. It's going to be a magical summer, she thought, skipping down the road to meet her friend.

The laird of Invercullion stared out the window. Damn, he thought. Damn and blast. His son was too like his mother and she was never up to much. It was a silly marriage, hasty and at his father's bidding. Now Roderick tells him, by letter no less, that he'll be home from university this weekend and is bringing with him the girl he's going to marry. They met while she was modelling at an evening art course he'd been attending. He's also thinking, he says, about enrolling in art school and hopes to become an artist. He has already secured a small commission to paint a mural in an Edinburgh pub, and more will surely follow. We'll see about that, thought the laird. And what did his wife say when he showed her the letter at breakfast. She bit on her toast, took a sip of tea, spooned a dollop of mashed egg into her mouth and rang for Elsie to make up the spare room. 'Master Roderick is bringing his fiancée home to meet us,' she said. Fiancée! Artist! We'll see about that!

Geordie wakened to the sound o the shipyerd whustle. Anither warkin day in Glescae, he thocht. And Big Alec wis efter him. It was aa ower the heid o that money tae. Jings. Wis it ony wonder he couldnae sleep. Weel, he'd slept a wee bit, but no very much. He looked at his bairns in their wee shirt tails, happily playing withoot a care in the warld, while ootside the windae dark cloods gaithered. His wife, Jinty, made their porridge and tea. It was aa they ever had, aa they could afford. He got up and streeched hissel, rollin a fag with the tea leaves he'd left to dry on the big kitchen range the nicht afore, mixed with the tobacco scrapings frae his jaikit pocket. He steppit ower the bairns and tellt Jinty he'd hae a bit breakfast in a meenit. Sittin on the stairheid cludgie he felt a draught come throw the broken windaes, saw the watter run down the wa's and heard the noise o the nearby hooses. Someone rattled the door. It was Mrs Thomson a puir auld buddy that was bad wi her nerves, never able tae get oot the bit. I'll no be a meenit Mrs T, he said. Well hurry up well, she replied, kindly. The persistent breeze made him think. A man deserves mair than this, but even if this is aa he haes, a man also haes his dignity. They could nivir tak that. Only he could loss it. A man must be able to face his bairns and his wife, his neebours and his freends, He must be able tae look them straicht in the face.

Big Alec! What Big Alec? He'd face him. He was ready.

So there we are then, a wholesome tale, dramatically told, with neither drugs, addiction, sex nor bad language anywhere in view. Obviously, I have only given a taster. This is just the beginning and the plot weaves its way round many themes and corners before we reach the final pages. As to the outcome, what happens next? I hear you ask; well, I fear I cannot continue further. One must be ever vigilant; there is, after all, no copyright on ideas.

I remain, sir,
Yours sincerely,
J. Maxwell Hastie.

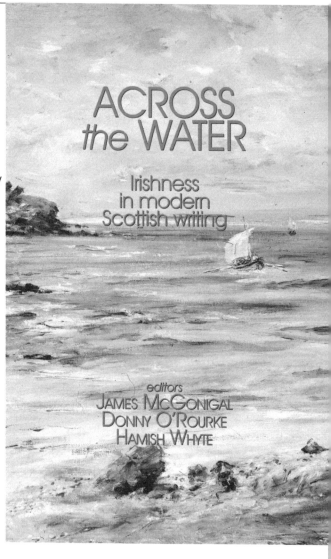

ACROSS
the WATER

Irishness
in modern
Scottish writing

editors
JAMES McGONIGAL
DONNY O'ROURKE
HAMISH WHYTE

Argyll
p u b l i s h i n g

1 902831 15 2 £9.99   June 2000
from bookshops and mail order
tel 01369 820229

DELIBERATELY THIRSTY
YOUR READING!

Next issue
7
(August 2000)

❑

Subscribe!
and get a FREE back issue of
Deliberately Thirsty

MAIL ORDER

THIS IS A CUT MARK BUT SHOULD YOU NOT WISH TO DEFACE YOUR DELIBERATELY THIRSTY BY CUTTING OUT THIS PAGE, PLEASE PHOTOCOPY OR JUST PHONE

CONTRIBUTORS

Leila Aboulela grew up in Khartoum and since 1990 has been living in Aberdeen. Her stories have been broadcast on BBC Radio and published in anthologies. Her first novel *The Translator* is published by Polygon.

Katherine Ashton lives and works in the Netherlands. She has completed two novels of a planned trilogy of which *Eve: Anatomy of a White Woman* is the first.

Alan Bissett was published in Macallan *Shorts* (1999) and his work has appeared in *Deliberately Thirsty* and *Cutting Teeth*. He admits that he still takes the occasional day shopping trip to Glasgow.

Ian Hunter is writer in residence with Alloa Young Writers.

Irene Leake is a sculptor drawn to writing by the lightness of its tools.

Carl MacDougall's most recent novel is *Stone Over Water* (Minerva).

Hilda Meers is the author of a ground-breaking work on language acquisition and a novel, *The Blood Tie* (Citron). She has lived on the Moray Firth for the last two years.

Helena Nelson makes excellent pastry and has three pet semicolons. She is extremely allergic to peanuts. (true).

Colm Quinn is from Belfast and currently lives in Aberdeen. His poetry has been widely published in magazines.

John Symons studied Chemistry at Oxford and successfully held out against joining the family business – the Inland Revenue. Retiring early from a career as an energy economist in London and Aberdeen, he is now economising his energy.

Paul Welsh is a playwright and filmmaker. He lives in Glasgow.

W.L. Wheatley is an American who lives in Massachusetts and works in film and TV production. He has written a novel called *A Crow Story* and his children's story *Mr Bumble and the Hippo* will be published this year.

DELIBERATELY THIRSTY
SEÁN BRADLEY EDITOR
www.deliberatelythirsty.com

REJECTION!

- ❏ We like it, but . . .
- ❏ We don't like it.
- ❏ We tried to like it.
- ❏ We don't have room for it.
- ❏ We lost it.
- ❏ The dog ate it.
- ❏ We liked the look of it, but not the smell.
- ❏ We liked you, but not it.
- ❏ We liked it, but not you.

- ❏ Send this to *The New Yorker* immediately.
- ❏ Send this to a psychiatrist immediately.
- ❏ Send money.

- ❏ Why are you writing like this?

- ❏ Oh gosh, we agree:
    - ❏ incest ❏ abuse
    - ❏ World War II ❏ the Thatcher years
    - are/were just *terrible*.

- ❏ We're too stupid to understand it.
- ❏ You're too stupid to understand it.
- ❏ We couldn't get it open.
- ❏ We never received it.

- ❏ We're hung over.

- ❏ It's ❏ too much ❏ not enough like
    - ❏ Lewis Grassic Gibbon ❏ Anne Tyler
    - ❏ Irvine Welsh ❏ Irvine Welsh ❏ Kathy Acker
- ❏ Thank you for the free paper clips.

LIKE ONE OF THESE